Dear Parent:

Congratulations! Your child is taking the first steps on an exciting journey. The destination? Independent reading!

STEP INTO READING® will help your child get there. The program offers five steps to reading success. Each step includes fun stories and colorful art. There are also Step into Reading Sticker Books, Step into Reading Math Readers, Step into Reading Phonics Readers, Step into Reading Write-In Readers, and Step into Reading Phonics Boxed Sets—a complete literacy program with something to interest every child.

Learning to Read, Step by Step!

Ready to Read   Preschool–Kindergarten
• big type and easy words • rhyme and rhythm • picture clues
For children who know the alphabet and are eager to begin reading.

Reading with Help   Preschool–Grade 1
• basic vocabulary • short sentences • simple stories
For children who recognize familiar words and sound out new words with help.

Reading on Your Own   Grades 1–3
• engaging characters • easy-to-follow plots • popular topics
For children who are ready to read on their own.

Reading Paragraphs   Grades 2–3
• challenging vocabulary • short paragraphs • exciting stories
For newly independent readers who read simple sentences with confidence.

Ready for Chapters   Grades 2–4
• chapters • longer paragraphs • full-color art
For children who want to take the plunge into chapter books but still like colorful pictures.

STEP INTO READING® is designed to give every child a successful reading experience. The grade levels are only guides. Children can progress through the steps at their own speed, developing confidence in their reading, no matter what their grade.

Remember, a lifetime love of reading starts with a single step!

A Princess Treasury

Visit us on the Web!
StepIntoReading.com
www.randomhouse.com/kids

Educators and librarians, for a variety of teaching tools, visit us at
www.randomhouse.com/teachers

ISBN: 978-0-7364-2772-2
Printed in the United States of America   10 9 8 7 6 5 4 3 2

STEP INTO READING®

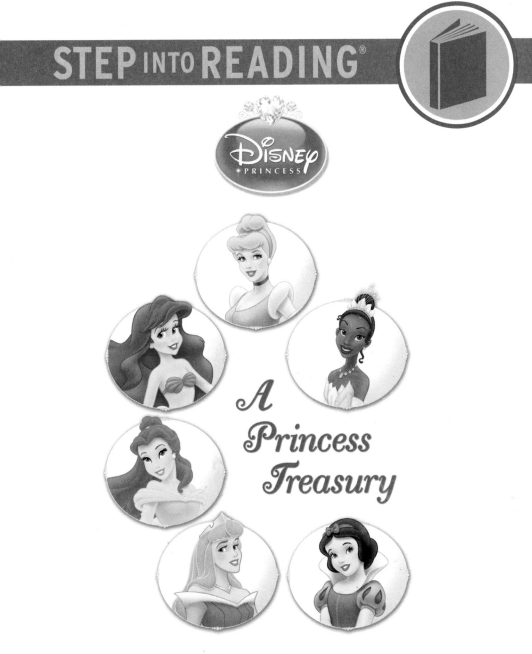

Disney PRINCESS

A Princess Treasury

Step 2 Books

A Collection of Six Early Readers

Random House New York

Contents

A Dream for a Princess

By Melissa Lagonegro
Illustrated by Pulsar Estudio

Random House 🏠 New York

There once was a girl
named Cinderella.
She was kind and gentle.

Cinderella lived with
her wicked Stepmother
and stepsisters.

She had many chores.

She served them tea.

She cooked their food.

She washed their clothes.

"Get my scarf!"

yelled one sister.

"Fix my dress!"

shouted the other.

They were very mean
to poor Cinderella.

One day,

a letter came

from the palace.

"Come meet the Prince

at a Royal Ball," it said.

The stepsisters
were very excited.
Cinderella was, too!

Cinderella dreamed of
wearing a fancy gown . . .

. . . and dancing with
the Prince.

Cinderella's Stepmother
gave her more chores.
Cinderella did not
have time to make
her ball gown.

"Surprise!"
cried her little friends.
They had made her
a fancy gown.

"Now I can go
to the ball!"
cheered Cinderella.

Oh, no!
The stepsisters
tore her gown.
It was ruined!

Cinderella cried.

Piff, puff, poof!

Her Fairy Godmother

appeared.

"You cannot go
to the ball
like that," she said.

She waved
her magic wand.
Poof!

A royal coach.

White horses.

Two coachmen.

And a beautiful gown!

Cinderella was headed
to the ball!

At the ball,
the Prince saw
Cinderella.

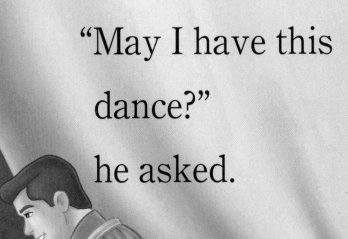

"May I have this
dance?"
he asked.

They danced . . .

. . . and danced . . .

. . . and danced.

Cinderella was so happy.
She was wearing
a fancy gown.

And she was dancing
with the Prince!

Her dream had come true!

DISNEP
PRINCESS

The
Sweetest Spring

By Apple Jordan

Illustrated by

Francesco Legramandi & Gabriella Matta

Random House 🏠 New York

Spring is here!

There is much to do.

Sweep the floors
and mop up, too.

Clean the windows.

Scrub the floor.

Dust the tables.

Wash the door.

Singing makes
the chores more fun.
One, two, three!
The work is done.

The house is ready
to welcome spring.
Sharing the chores
is the sweetest thing.

Winter is over.

Now it is spring.

Ariel and her sisters

sing for the king.

Everyone gathers
to see all the flowers.

They dance and sing

for hours and hours.

The salt water is warm.

It smells of spring.

A springtime fair

is the sweetest thing.

Spring is here!
Jasmine has one wish—
to see a spring shower.
Splish-splash-splish!

Rain showers are

a sure sign

it is spring.

Splashing in puddles
is the sweetest thing.

Spring is here!

Wake up, friends!

The winter slumber
has come to an end.

A robin comes out
to sing a spring song.
The bumblebees are
buzzing right along.

The animals are happy.

At last it is spring.

Greeting our friends

is the sweetest thing.

Cinderella and her prince
share a spring stroll.
They see a rabbit
peeking out of its hole.

Flowers bud.
Roses bloom.
Wedding bells ring
for this new
bride and groom.

The happy couple shares
the wonders of spring.

Springtime love
is the sweetest thing.

Belle makes a garden.
There is much to do.

She wants plants
and pretty flowers, too.

She plants some seeds,
all in a row.

The soil
needs water.
It helps
flowers grow.

Belle waits . . .

and waits . . .

for days and hours.

The garden has grown
many pretty flowers.

The yard is filled with
the flowers of spring.
Planting a garden
is the sweetest thing!

THE
PRINCESS
AND THE
FROG

Kiss the Frog

By Melissa Lagonegro

Illustrated by Elizabeth Tate, Caroline LaVelle Egan,
Studio IBOIX, Michael Inman, and the Disney
Storybook Artists

Random House 🏠 New York

Tiana works hard.
She has no time
for fun.

She has a dream.

She wants to own

a restaurant.

Prince Naveen
likes to have fun.

72

He loves music.

He visits New Orleans.

Facilier is a bad man.
He plans to trick
Naveen.

Facilier uses bad magic.

He turns Prince Naveen

into a frog!

Tiana goes
to a costume party.
She wishes on a star.
She wishes
for her restaurant.
Naveen sees her.

Tiana meets Naveen.
She looks like a princess.
Naveen thinks her kiss
will make him human.
He wants to kiss Tiana.

Tiana kisses Naveen.
But she is not
a real princess.

The kiss does not work!

Naveen is still a frog.

Tiana turns

into a frog,

too!

Tiana and Naveen
get lost.
They do not like
being frogs.
They do not like
each other.

They meet

Louis the alligator.

Naveen has fun!

Tiana does not.

The frogs try
to catch a bug.
They get stuck together.

Ray is a firefly.

He helps the frogs.

They all become friends.

Tiana shows Naveen
how to cook.

They like
each other now.

Tiana and Naveen
find Mama Odie.

She makes good magic.

She can help them.

Mama Odie

shows Naveen

a princess.

He must kiss her.

Then he and Tiana will

become human again!

Tiana and Naveen

are happy!

They are in love.

Naveen kisses a princess.

But it is too late.

The spell does not break!

Naveen is still a frog.

Tiana is still a frog.

Tiana and Naveen
are happy!
They are in love.

Naveen kisses a princess.

But it is too late.

The spell does not break!

Naveen is still a frog.

Tiana is still a frog.

Tiana and Prince Naveen
go back to Mama Odie.
They get married.

Now Tiana is
a <u>real</u> princess.
They kiss. <u>POOF!</u>
They become human again!

Tiana's dream comes true.

She gets her restaurant.

She has love.

She has everything
she needs!

STEP INTO READING®

STEP 2

DISNEY
PRINCESS

The
Perfect Dress

By Melissa Lagonegro
Illustrated by Elisa Marrucchi

Random House 🏠 New York

Dust and dirt

make a mess!

Cinderella needs
a brand-new dress.

Clean and bright.
Oh, what fun!

This blue dress is
the perfect one.

Jasmine must choose
a skirt or a gown.

Her friend Rajah
looks on with a frown.

Jasmine and Aladdin
enjoy a starry night!

Her green outfit
is truly just right.

Belle is excited about
the fancy feast!

Her green outfit
is truly just right.

Belle is excited about
the fancy feast!

She gets dressed for
her date with the Beast.

Belle and the Beast

share a night of romance.

Her yellow gown is
perfect for this dance.

Everyone sings in
the wedding parade!

King Triton sends off
his little mermaid!

Ariel's wedding dress
fits just right.

Prince Eric thinks she looks lovely in white!

Sleeping Beauty has
such a busy day!

The fairies can help.

They are on their way!

Music and menus.
There is much to do.

Should Aurora's dress be pink or dark blue?

The Prince arrives with
his horse by his side.

Snow White must dress
for their royal ride.

It's chilly and windy.
It feels like a storm.

A blue and red cape will
keep Snow White warm.

Slip on the shoes.

A blue and red cape will
keep Snow White warm.

Slip on the shoes.

Fluff up the dress.

Put on the jewelry.

Look your best.

Which one do you think
is the perfect dress?

Sealed with a Kiss

by Melissa Lagonegro
illustrated by Elisa Marrucchi

Random House 🏠 New York

Ariel and Flounder
love to play
hide-and-seek
under the sea.

They want the baby seal
to play with them.
Ariel points
to where the seal
could be.

The two friends swim to find him.

They find the seal!
He is sitting
on a rock.
He cannot wait
to play hide-and-seek.

"One, two, three . . . ,"
Ariel starts to count.
The others hide.

"Ready or not,
here I come,"
she says.

Ariel looks
in the seaweed.
She searches
in the sea plants.

"Gotcha!"
cries Ariel.
She has found
Flounder!

Now Ariel
has to find
the baby seal.

Where can he be?

She looks
inside a chest.
She sees many things.
But no baby seal.

Now Ariel
has to find
the baby seal.

Where can he be?

She looks
inside a chest.
She sees many things.
But no baby seal.

Ariel looks

under a rock cliff.

She sees

a sleeping blowfish.

But no baby seal.

Ariel hears music.
She sees fish
dancing and singing.
But no baby seal!

Ariel even goes
back to the rock.

She sees Scuttle.

But <u>no</u> baby seal!

Squeak! Squeak!

"What is that noise?"

asks Ariel.

They swim
to find out.

Oh, no!

It is the baby seal.

He is stuck!

His tail is caught

in a giant clamshell.

Ariel tries

to open the shell.

She lifts!

She pulls!

She does it!
Ariel sets
the seal free!

Ariel is happy
she has found
the seal.
And the seal
is <u>very</u> happy
to be found.

Ariel gives

her friend

a big hug.

She seals it
with a kiss!

STEP INTO READING®

STEP 2

DISNEY
PRINCESS

Ballerina Princess

By Melissa Lagonegro

Illustrated by Niall Harding

Random House New York

A princess loves
to dream
about dancing.

She spins.

She twirls.

She moves
as if she is
floating on air.

Snow White meets
a handsome prince.

The happy couple
dances and spins.

What a lovely pair!

Belle has sweet
dancing dreams.

Belle stands
on her toes.
She holds her
arms high.

She leaps
into the air.

Belle shines
like a star.
Her dress sparkles.

One leg is up.

One leg is down.

She holds her pose.

Aurora daydreams
about her
dancing costume.

Should she wear

a tutu or a gown?

Cinderella dances
at the royal ball
in her dreams.

She twirls and whirls
across the floor.

Prince Charming

watches

Cinderella.

The Prince takes
her hand.
He asks her to dance.

They glide
across the room.
The guests
clap and cheer.

Ariel dreams
about dancing
with Prince Eric.
If only she had feet!

Spin and twirl
and jump!

Turn and leap
and prance!

A princess loves
to dance!